Blue Dot Kids Press

www.BlueDotKidsPress.com

Original English-language edition published in 2022 by Blue Dot Kids Press,

P.O. Box 2344, San Francisco, CA 94126. Blue Dot Kids Press is a trademark of Blue Dot Publications LLC.

Original English-language edition © 2022 Blue Dot Publications LLC

Original English-language edition translation © 2022 Johanna McCalmont

Published under exclusive license with Camelozampa.

Italian-language edition originally published under the title: *Avrò cura di te*. © Camelozampa, Italy, 2021

Original English-language edition edited by Summer Dawn Laurie and designed by Teresa Bonaddio

BLUE D●T KIDS PRESS

Cataloging in Publication Data is available from the United States Library of Congress.

ISBN: 9781737603238

The illustrations in this book were made with acrylic paint and collage.

Printed in China with soy inks.

First Printing

Maria Loretta Giraldo   Nicoletta Bertelle

Translated by Johanna McCalmont

I'll Take Care of You

BLUE DOT KIDS PRESS

Once
there was
a tiny seed.
So small in the
great big world,
it felt lost and
lonely.

The Sky, the Water, and the Earth saw it,
and their hearts bloomed.

The Earth said to the seed,
"Don't be afraid. I'll take care of you."
And welcomed it into its sweet, soft soil.

The Water said to the seed,

"Don't be afraid. I'll take care of you."

And watered it with crystal clear droplets of rain.

The Sky said to the seed,

"Don't be afraid. I'll take care of you."

And made the bright, warm sun rise.

The seed took heart.

It grew and became
a tiny shoot.

It grew and became
a sapling.

It grew and eventually became

a magnificent leafy tree in full bloom.

One day a single bird arrived, a tiny blackcap.

The tree saw how lost and lonely the little bird looked and said,

"Stay here and build your nest in my branches. I'll take care of you."

The blackcap took heart.
She built her nest in the branches
of the tree and felt safe and protected.
One day she laid an egg.
She sat on it patiently until the shell cracked
and a tiny chick hatched.
"I'll take care of you," said the blackcap.
She kept it warm and taught it
how to sing and fly.

When the time came, the chick grew strong and left the nest.

The blossoms on the tree lost their petals and slowly turned into apples.

Then the time came when all the apples were gone from the tree—all but one.

Soon, it too fell and split open, releasing the seeds it contained.
The Wind came and carried them away.
It scattered all the seeds where they would
be cared for by the Earth, the Sky, and the Water.

All but one. One seed fell among the rocks,
without any soil, sun, or rain.
The tree's crown hung as it wept for the dying seed.
"Don't worry. I'll take care of our tiny one,"
said the blackcap.

Quickly, she swooped down from her nest in the tree.

Carefully, she picked up the tiny seed in her beak and gave it to the Earth.

Patiently, she waited, hoping it would grow,
singing with all her heart . . .

. . . until
one day
she saw a
tiny shoot
appear.